Emily Arnold McCully

School

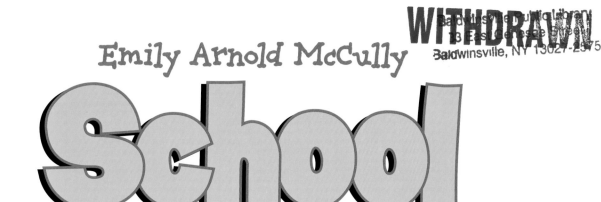

HarperCollinsPublishers

For Harriet

School
Copyright © 2005 by Emily Arnold McCully
Manufactured in China by South China Printing Company Ltd.
www.harperchildrens.com

Library of Congress Cataloging-in-Publication Data
McCully, Emily Arnold.
 School / Emily Arnold McCully.—1st ed.
  p.   cm.
Originally published without text: HarperCollins, 1987.
Summary: A curious little mouse decides to find out what school is all about.
ISBN 0-06-623856-0 — ISBN 0-06-623857-9 (lib. bdg.)
[1. Mice—Fiction. 2. Schools—Fiction.] I. Title.
PZ7.M13913Sc 2005   [E]—dc21   2003050847
Typography by Matt Adamec
1 2 3 4 5 6 7 8 9 10
❖
First Edition

School time!

Bitty thinks Mama won't miss her.

Everyone is busy.

"Sit here, Bitty."

"who knows the answer?"

"Go on, tell the class your answer."

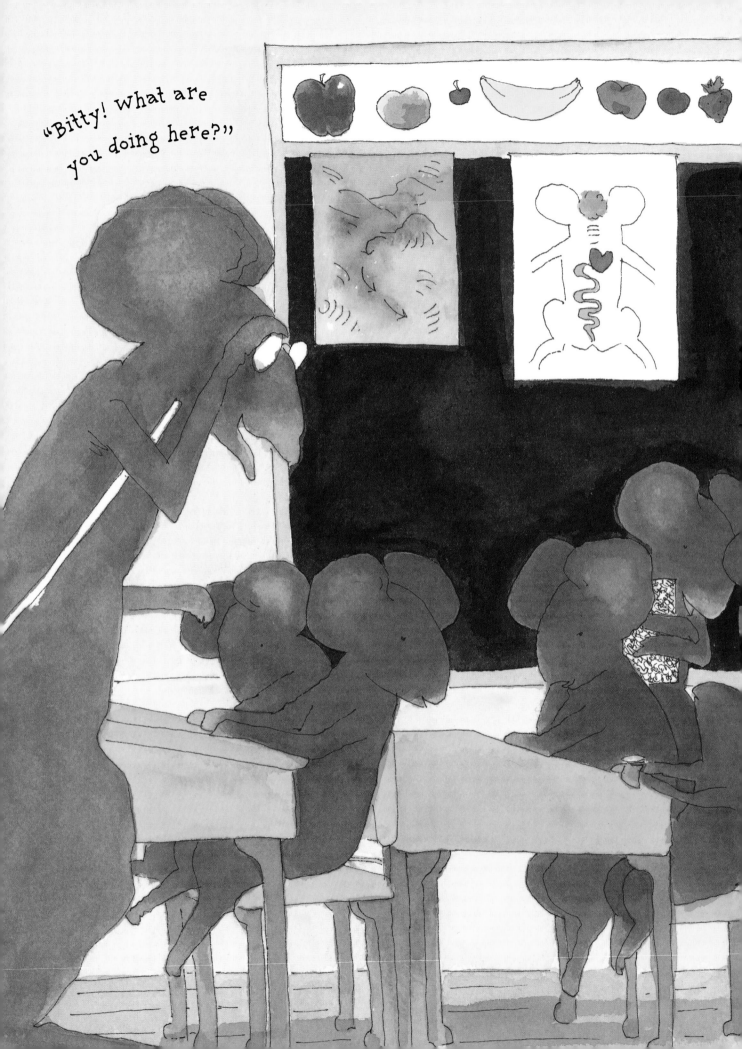

"Well, never mind. You can be my helper."

The class adds the acorns.

"Hello? Your Bitty has come to school!"

Snack time!

"Pass the juice, please, Bitty."

Story time!

"A-picnicking we go . . ."

Bitty falls asleep.

"Where's my baby?"

Mama is so happy to see Bitty.

Everyone waves good-bye.

"And Mama, then we did addition and
subtraction, and then we had . . ."